W9-CXN-794

Boogalaboo Meets Ranger Bob

By Doris Moore Marvin

Olive Branch Publishing, LLC

This book is published in remembrance of Olive Mae Moore.

Library of Congress Catalog Card Number: 2007921638

Library of Congress Cataloging in Publication Data

Marvin, Doris Moore
        The Adventures of Boogalaboo
        Boogalaboo Meets Ranger Bob

Illustrated by Charlie Cummings
Layout Design by Irma Mason

Summary: Boogalaboo, a small gray squirrel is separated from his family after a forest fire destroys his home. On his journey to find them, he is befriended by Ranger Bob who tries to keep the little squirrel out of trouble.

ISBN 13: 978-0-9793147-0-4
ISBN 10: 0-9793147-0-4

For Amber Lyn Marvin
who inspired me to write the
Boogalaboo stories.

"You warm my heart."

This is the story about a beautiful gray squirrel named Boogalaboo. Boogalaboo is always smiling, and his eyes twinkle like the stars. He isn't very big, but he has a very large gray and white tail that is very fluffy. When the sun shines on it just right you can see streaks of gold.

Some of the squirrels tease Boogalaboo because he stands at the mirror for hours combing his tail until it is soft and shiny. He doesn't like to brag, but he is very proud of his tail.

Everyone likes Boogalaboo because he is a good friend, and he has a kind heart. However, he is always getting into trouble.

He doesn't look for trouble —
trouble finds him.

Last winter Boogalaboo received new skates for Christmas. He could hardly wait to try them out on the frozen pond behind his house. When he got to the pond he was so excited he didn't notice the sign that read:

Danger—Keep Off the Ice!

Boogalaboo was skating about five minutes when he saw the ice cracking around his feet. He tried to skate away, but the ice broke and he fell into the icy cold water. Lucky for him his daddy came along and fished him out of the water by his tail. Boogalaboo caught a cold and spent the next week in bed.

Boogalaboo loves to eat strawberries and nuts. He likes all nuts, but his favorite is the pecan. He gathers them in his pouch, and then eats them one after the other until there are none left in the bag. Sometimes he eats so many, the bottom button on his shirt pops off, and then he usually gets a tummy ache.

*He doesn't look for trouble —
trouble finds him.*

As a matter of fact, getting into trouble is how Boogalaboo met Ranger Bob.

Ranger Bob is a forest ranger. He has been protecting the trees and the animals in the forest for over ten years. He is very tall and wears a hat that covers his curly red hair. His uniform is decorated with many badges and shiny medals.

He often goes to the elementary school to talk to the children about fire safety. They love for him to bring his animal friends, like the baby raccoon he rescued from a hunter's trap in the forest.

Ranger Bob met Boogalaboo the day a fire was spotted on the east side of the forest. As soon as the alarm sounded, he hurried out the door of the ranger station and jumped into his bright yellow truck. He drove very quickly, but carefully, down the winding trails of the forest. He could see several of the animals scurrying for safety.

At the bottom of the hill he could see the fire trucks spraying water on the last of the burning trees. The firemen and Ranger Bob worked for hours making sure the fire would not return.

Several trees were destroyed that day, and many animals lost their homes because a camper was not careful with his campfire. A man driving a large white van saved many of the animals by taking them to safer locations.

One of the trees that burned was one Ranger Bob climbed when he was a little boy. He was so sorry this tree burned because he had such good memories of it. His daddy told him this tree was special because the entire forest could be seen from the top branch.

Ranger Bob's daddy had taken him for long walks in the forest when he was a small child. They would stop and sit under the shade of the tree and have lunch, and talk about many things.

He always smiled when he thought of them sitting under this tree, but today he was not smiling. As a matter of fact, one single tear rolled down Ranger Bob's cheek. He knew he would not be able to sit under the tree again, and that made him very sad.

At one time, a family of squirrels lived in the tree. Ranger Bob hoped they all got out before the fire started.

It had been a very long day, and it was time for Ranger Bob to go back to the ranger station. As he was getting into his truck he heard a noise coming from behind the bushes. Imagine his surprise when he saw a little squirrel lying on the ground.

The little squirrel was coughing and struggling to take a breath. He was covered with dirt and soot from the fire. Beside the squirrel was a tiny little teddy bear.

Ranger Bob bent down to pick up the squirrel and asked him, "What is your name little fellow?" The squirrel looked up at Ranger Bob and tried to tell him his name, but he could hardly talk because of the smoke. He tried again, and then very softly said, "My name is Boogalaboo. Where are my mommy and daddy, and my little sister? Mommy told me to follow her when the fire started, but I went back up the tree to get my teddy bear."

Ranger Bob told him he didn't know where they were, but he would try to find them. That was the last thing Boogalaboo heard as his head fell over onto Ranger Bob's chest. He was fast asleep from exhaustion.

Ranger Bob knew there was something special about this little squirrel with the funny name. He decided to take him to the ranger station and nurse him back to health.

After the fire, Boogalaboo's tail was no longer soft and fluffy. It was burned and some of the hair had come out. He was very worried his tail would never be the same as it was before.

Ranger Bob told him the hair would grow back, but he would have to be patient. Boogalaboo has never been a very patient squirrel, but he said he would try.

Boogalaboo lived at the ranger station for several months. He was feeling much better now, thanks to his good friend.

Every day they would drive through the forest making sure the animals and trees were safe. He liked riding in the big yellow truck with Ranger Bob.

PLEASE
BE CAREFUL
WITH
CAMPFIRES

No one knew what happened to Boogalaboo's family. Were they able to get out of the forest? Boogalaboo said he would never give up trying to find them.

Ranger Bob realized very early that Boogalaboo had a way of getting into trouble. He was curious about everything, and sometimes that curiosity would get him into trouble—like the time he was helping him with a few chores.

While they were gathering fire wood, Boogalaboo saw a skunk behind a tree at the edge of the fire station. Now, as we all know, it is not a good idea to surprise a skunk.

However, Boogalaboo didn't think about that when he pranced over to him with a big smile on his face. He was sure the skunk would want to be his friend. The skunk did not know him and ran away, but <u>not</u> before spraying Boogalaboo.

Poor Boogalaboo, he didn't look for trouble — trouble found him.

Boogalaboo was very upset and he started to cry. Ranger Bob said he would help him get the skunk smell off, but it would take a lot of bathing.

They walked down to the river carrying a bath brush, towels and several bars of soap. After many hours and much scrubbing, he was starting to smell better.

It's a good thing Boogalaboo didn't look up in the tree above his head, because he would have seen that little skunk giggling at him.

Boogalaboo enjoyed staying at the ranger station, but he knew it was time to find a home of his own. It was not going to be easy telling his friend goodbye.

Boogalaboo wanted to do something special for Ranger Bob before he left, so he planted a tree to replace the one that burned.

Ranger Bob was very happy to see what Boogalaboo had done. He was also surprised to see the basket of goodies Boogalaboo prepared for a picnic by the new tree.

They ate peanut butter sandwiches,
walnut pancakes, strawberries and cheese.
They drank lemonade and had pecan pie
for dessert.

The old tree had good memories for Ranger
Bob and Boogalaboo, but they were starting
to make good memories with the <u>new</u> tree.

On a very beautiful spring morning Boogalaboo was packing the last of his clothes in his little green suitcase. He was wearing the new blue shirt Ranger Bob bought him as a going-away present.

He was smiling as he looked in the mirror admiring his beautiful fluffy tail that <u>had</u> grown back. Actually, he thought it was even more soft and fluffy than it had been before.

Today he would be leaving to find his new home. He didn't know where, but he knew it would be in a very tall beautiful tree.

Ranger Bob told Boogalaboo he would miss him, and to let him know if he ever needs help. Boogalaboo said, "Thank you, Ranger Bob, for everything you have done for me."

Boogalaboo turned and waved at Ranger Bob as he walked down the long winding trail toward his new home. He was a little scared, but he was mostly excited to start on this new adventure.

As Ranger Bob watched Boogalaboo go around the bend, he somehow knew he would be getting Boogalaboo out of trouble many, many times in days to come.

Because as we all know,

Boogalaboo doesn't look for trouble — trouble finds him!

Coming Soon!

Book Two

"Boogalaboo Finds a Home"